KU-799-119

and the

MOST ANNOYING FAIRY

For Sylvie
R.I.

For Finley and Fred
K.M.

ORCHARD BOOKS

First published in Great Britain in 2016 by The Watts Publishing Group

1 3 5 7 9 10 8 6 4 2

Text © Rose Impey 2016

Illustrations © Katharine McEwen 2016

The moral rights of the author and illustrator have been asserted.
All characters and events in this publication, other than those clearly in the public domain, are fictitious and any resemblance to real persons, living or dead, is purely coincidental.

All rights reserved.
No part of this publication may be reproduced, stored in a retrieval system, or transmitted, in any form or by any means, without the prior permission in writing of the publisher, nor be otherwise circulated in any form of binding or cover other than that in which it is published and without a similar condition including this condition being imposed on the subsequent purchaser.

A CIP catalogue record for this book is available from the British Library.

ISBN 978 1 40832 522 3 (HB)
ISBN 978 1 40832 528 5 (PB)

Printed in China

The paper and board used in this book are made from wood from responsible sources

Orchard Books
An imprint of Hachette Children's Group
Part of The Watts Publishing Group Limited
Carmelite House, 50 Victoria Embankment, London EC4Y 0DZ

An Hachette UK Company
www.hachette.co.uk
www.hachettechildrens.co.uk

CUMBRIA LIBRARIES
3 8003 04764 4521

YOUNG PEOPLES LIBRARY SERVICES
Cumbria County Council
Libraries, books and more.....

12/10
ULVERSTON
14 MAR 2017
- 4 AUG 2018
28 JAN 2019
21 JUN 2019
03 SEP 2019
Returned to stock 1/8/23
WITHDRAWN FROM CIRCULATION

Please return/renew this item by the last date shown.
Library items may also be renewed by phone on
030 33 33 1234 (24hours) or via our website

www.cumbria.gov.uk/libraries

Cumbria Libraries
CLIC
Interactive Catalogue

Ask for a CLIC password

and the

MOST ANNOYING FAIRY

Rose Impey · Katharine McEwen

ORCHARD

Cast of Characters

Sir Lance-a-Little

Harold the Horse

Princess Plum

Huffalot the Dragon

The Most Annoying Fairy

Sir Lance-a-Little paced up and down outside the dragon's cave. He'd been there *for ages*, waiting to fight his No. 1 enemy.

The dragon had challenged *him* to a fight this time.

So Sir Lance-a-Little had come, *immediately*.

But the dragon
still hadn't appeared.
Annoyingly, Sir Lance-a-Little's
cousin, Princess Plum, had
appeared, though. "Did I miss
the fight?" she asked, puffing.

"No!" shouted Sir Lance-a-Little, very loudly, hoping Huffalot would hear. "Because that cowardly dragon won't come out!"

The only reply was a low rumbling noise that sounded like someone groaning, "Go awaayyy." But Sir Lance-a-Little had come to fight and he wasn't going anywhere.

"Coming, ready or not!" he warned the dragon. Holding out his sharp sword, he marched bravely into the mouth of the cave.

But he quickly came out again,
followed by huge gusts of fire.
Much more clearly this time,
they heard the dragon roar,
"I said, go away!"

"Maybe he's poorly," Princess Plum suggested.

"Poorly!" said Sir Lance-a-Little. "He's a *dragon*!"

But when the dragon finally appeared he asked, more sympathetically, "I say, Huffalot, is something wrong?"

"Toothache!" groaned Huffalot. "Could you come back tomorrow?"

Sir Lance-a-Little was disappointed, of course. But he was far too honourable to take advantage of a poorly dragon.

He turned and set off home in a bad mood, with Princess Plum riding behind him.

"I could fight you," she offered.

But Sir Lance-a-Little ignored her. Brave knights fought dragons, not their irritating younger cousins.

On the way home they met a Most Annoying Fairy.

Sir Lance-a-Little could tell that she was going to be annoying because she looked a lot like his cousin. She sounded like her, too.

"You can have *three* wishes," the fairy said. "You'll have to be quick, though, I'm in a hurry. And only three, that's the rule, OK?"

But before Sir Lance-a-Little had time to choose, Princess Plum had made a first wish.

"I wish I had a suit of armour."

"Princesses don't wear armour!"

the Most Annoying Fairy

pointed out.

"They *might*, if they had any,"
said Princess Plum.
The fairy couldn't really argue
with that. "*Whatever*," she said
grumpily, waving her wand.

Hey presto … There stood Princess Plum, in a full suit of armour, looking very pleased with herself.

Quickly, Sir Lance-a-Little chose a wish of his own. "I wish I had a sword—" he began.

"You've got a sword!" the fairy interrupted.

"*Big enough and sharp enough,*" Sir Lance-a-Little continued, "*to cut off a dragon's head with one stroke!*" Again the fairy grumpily waved her wand.

Hey presto … Sir Lance-a-Little stood there with a huge gleaming sword, much bigger than his own. Now, if only he had someone to fight with it.

Suddenly he knew what else to wish for. But too late ...

"I wish I had a sword ..." said Princess Plum, "*and* a shield ... and a spear ... and a lance ... and a horse of my own!"

"Just stop right there," said the fairy. "You know the rules ..."

Quickly, Sir Lance-a-Little said, "I wish you'd cure the dragon's toothache."

The fairy waved her wand in the air. "*Whatever!*" she said, grumpily.

Hey presto … When they reached Huffalot's cave, the dragon was waiting for them, looking as fierce, and as cunning, as any dragon in the whole of Notalot. And not at all poorly …

Until he caught sight of Sir Lance-a-Little's gleaming new sword. It looked sharp enough, surely, to cut off a dragon's head with one stroke.

Suddenly, Huffalot didn't feel at all well. He clutched his stomach and groaned, "Ohhhhh! Ahhhhh!"

"Now what?" Sir Lance-a-Little asked, crossly.

"*Stomach ache,*" moaned Huffalot. "Must be *someone* I've eaten."

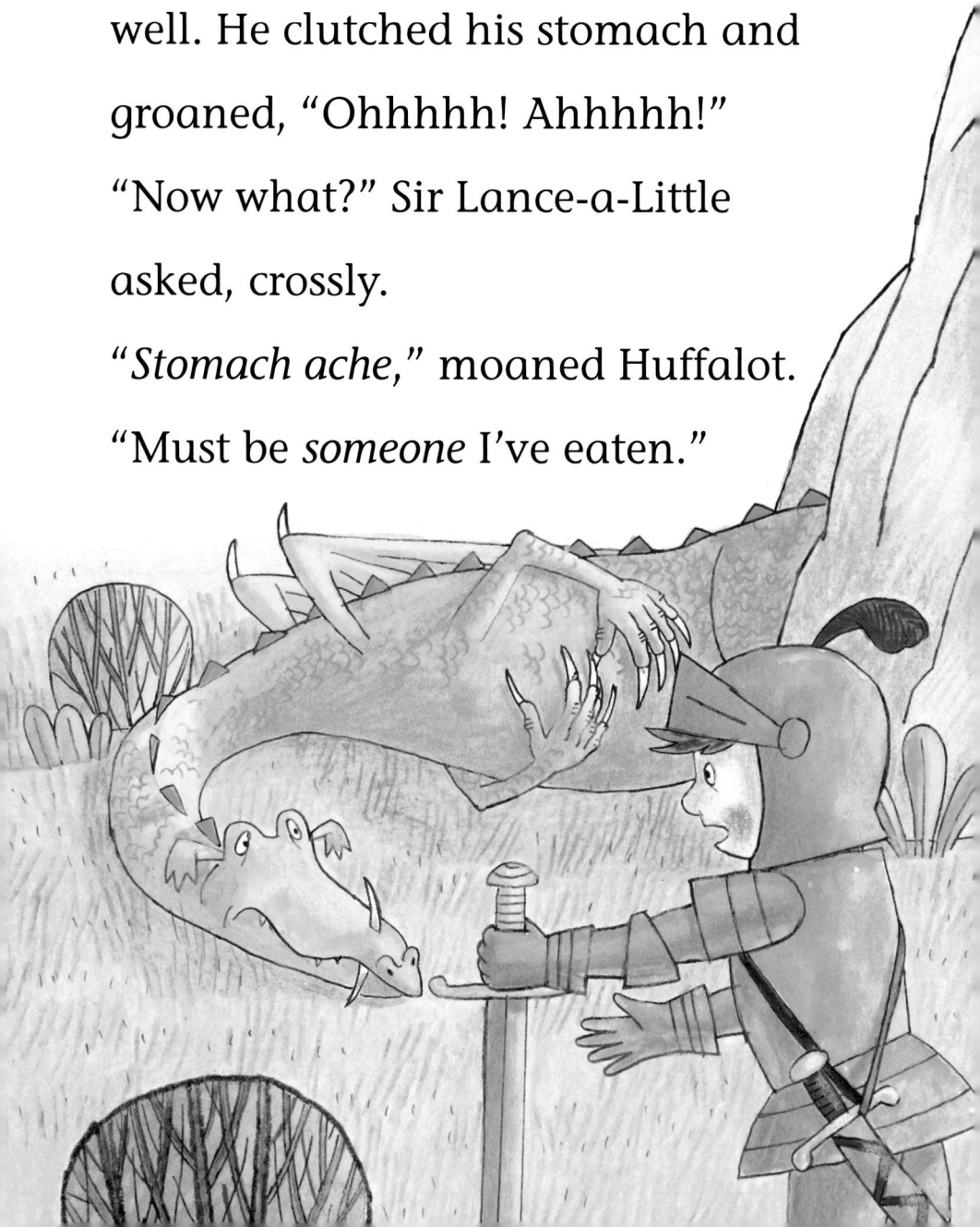

And, before Sir Lance-a-Little could stop him, the dragon disappeared into his cave.

The little knight was disappointed, of course, but he was far too honourable to fight a *sickly* dragon. Even one only *pretending* to be sick!

"I'll be back," he shouted into the cave. "Await my challenge!"

And next time he would show

Huffalot, *once and for all,* who was

the bravest and the best.

His name was …

Sir Lance-a-Little!

Join the bravest knight in Notalot for all his adventures!

Written by Rose Impey • Illustrated by Katharine McEwen

❑ Sir Lance-a-Little and the Big Bad Wolf	978 1 40832 520 9 (HB) 978 1 40832 526 1 (PB)
❑ Sir Lance-a-Little and the Three Angry Bears	978 1 40832 521 6 (HB) 978 1 40832 527 8 (PB)
❑ Sir Lance-a-Little and the Most Annoying Fairy	978 1 40832 522 3 (HB) 978 1 40832 528 5 (PB)
❑ Sir Lance-a-Little and the Terribly Ugly Troll	978 1 40832 523 0 (HB) 978 1 40832 529 2 (PB)
❑ Sir Lance-a-Little and the Ginormous Giant	978 1 40832 524 7 (HB) 978 1 40832 530 8 (PB)
❑ Sir Lance-a-Little and the Very Wicked Witch	978 1 40832 525 4 (HB) 978 1 40832 531 5 (PB)

Orchard Books are available from all good bookshops, or can be ordered from our website:
www.orchardbooks.co.uk
or telephone 01235 400400, or fax 01235 400454.

Prices and availability are subject to change.